Easter cooking

Rebecca Gilpin and Catherine Atkinson

Designed by Non Figg

Cover design and illustration by Katrina Fearn
Illustrated by Molly Sage
Photographs by Howard Allman

Contents

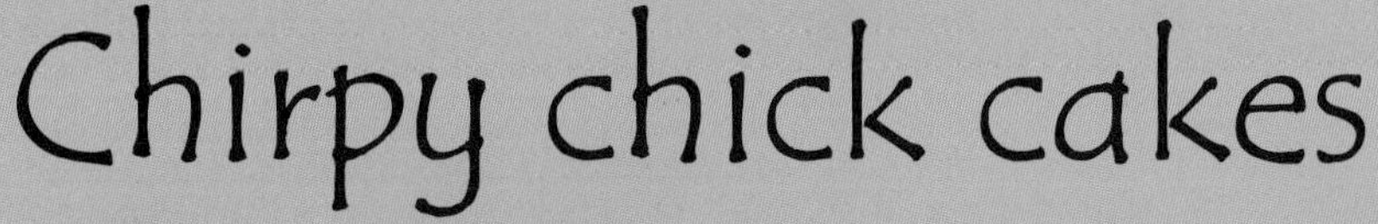

Chirpy chick cakes

To make 8 cakes, you will need:

50g (2oz) self-raising flour
1 medium egg
50g (2oz) caster sugar
50g (2oz) soft margarine
paper cake cases
a baking tray with shallow pans
small round sweets and jelly diamonds or slices

For the lemon butter icing:
40g (1½oz) butter, softened
75g (3oz) icing sugar, sifted
1 teaspoon of lemon juice (from a bottle or squeezed from a lemon)
1 drop of yellow food colouring

Heat your oven to 190°C, 375°F, gas mark 5, before you start.

The cakes need to be stored in an airtight container and eaten within three days.

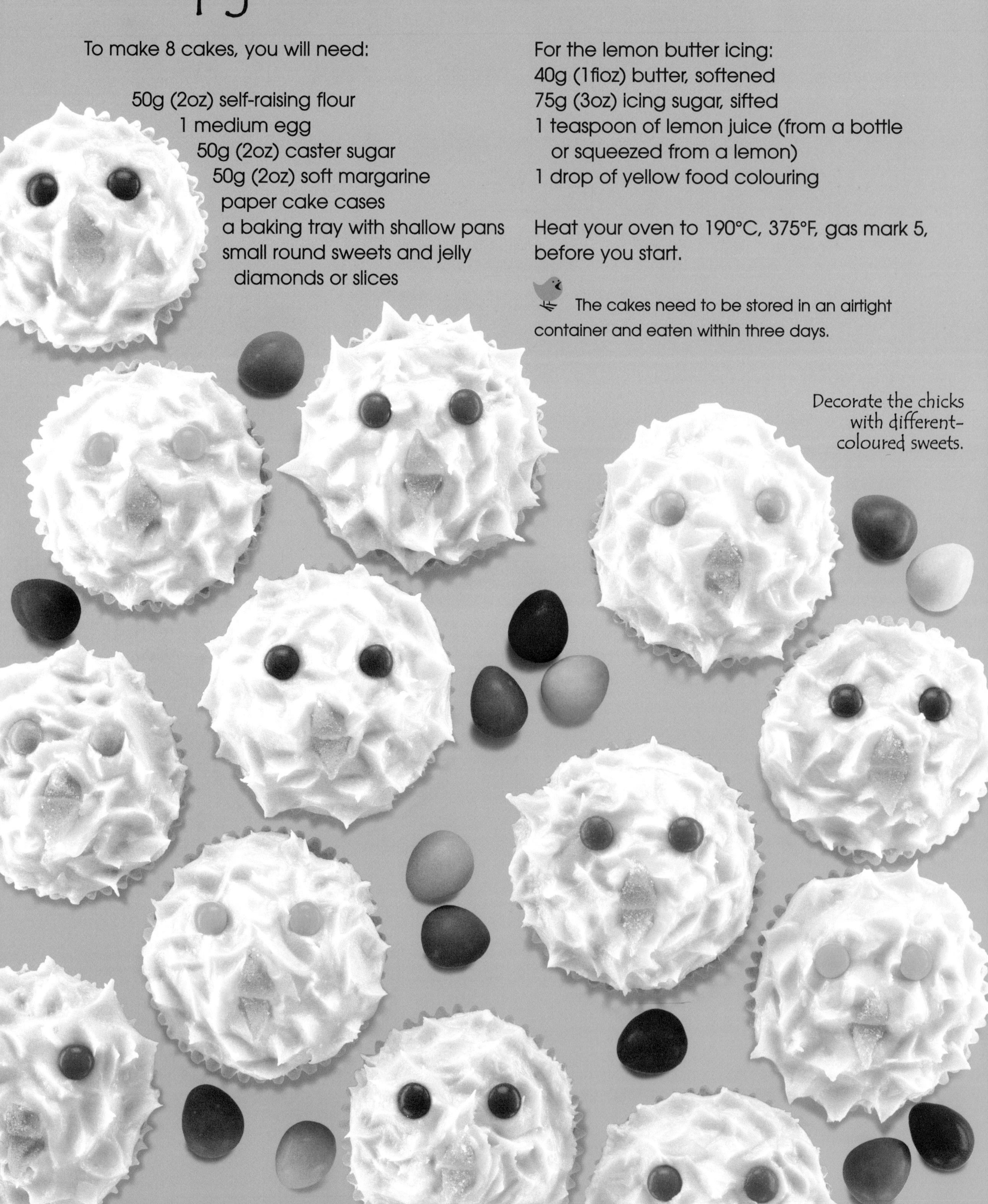

Decorate the chicks with different-coloured sweets.

1. Sift the flour through a sieve into a bowl. Break the egg into a cup, then add it to the flour. Add the sugar and margarine.

2. Beat the mixture firmly with a wooden spoon, until it is light and fluffy. Put eight paper cases into pans in the baking tray.

3. Using a teaspoon, half fill each paper case with the mixture. Then, bake the cakes in the oven for 18-20 minutes.

Bake the cakes until they are golden brown.

4. Take the cakes out of the oven. After a few minutes, lift them out of the baking tray and put them on a rack to cool.

5. For the icing, put the butter into a bowl. Beat it with a wooden spoon until it is creamy. Then, stir in half of the icing sugar.

6. Add the lemon juice, yellow food colouring and the rest of the icing sugar. Mix everything together well.

7. Using a blunt knife, cover the top of each cake with butter icing. Then, use a fork to make the icing look feathery.

8. Press two small round sweets onto each cake for the eyes. Then, cut eight jelly diamonds or slices in half for the beaks.

9. Press two halves into the icing on each cake, to make a beak. Make the pointed ends of the halves stick up a little.

Flower sweets

To make about 40 flowers, you will need:

225g (8oz) icing sugar
1 tablespoon of lemon juice (from a bottle or squeezed from a lemon)
2 teaspoons egg white, mixed from dried egg white (mix as directed on the packet)
2-3 drops of lemon essence
small jelly sweets
a small flower-shaped cutter
a baking sheet

The flower sweets need to be stored in an airtight container, on layers of greaseproof paper. Eat them within a week.

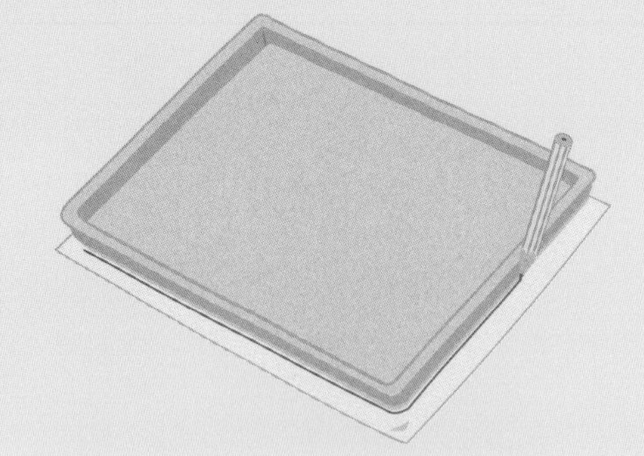

1. Put the baking sheet on a piece of greaseproof paper. Draw around the tin and cut out the shape. Put the shape in the tin.

2. Sift the icing sugar through a sieve into a large bowl. Make a hole in the middle of the icing sugar with a spoon.

If the mixture is a little dry, add a drop of water.

3. Mix the lemon juice, egg white and lemon essence in a small bowl. Pour them into the hole in the sugar. Stir them with a blunt knife.

4. Keep stirring everything together until the mixture starts to make a ball. Then, squeeze it between your fingers until it is smooth.

5. Sprinkle a little icing sugar onto a clean work surface. Sprinkle some onto a rolling pin too, to stop the mixture sticking.

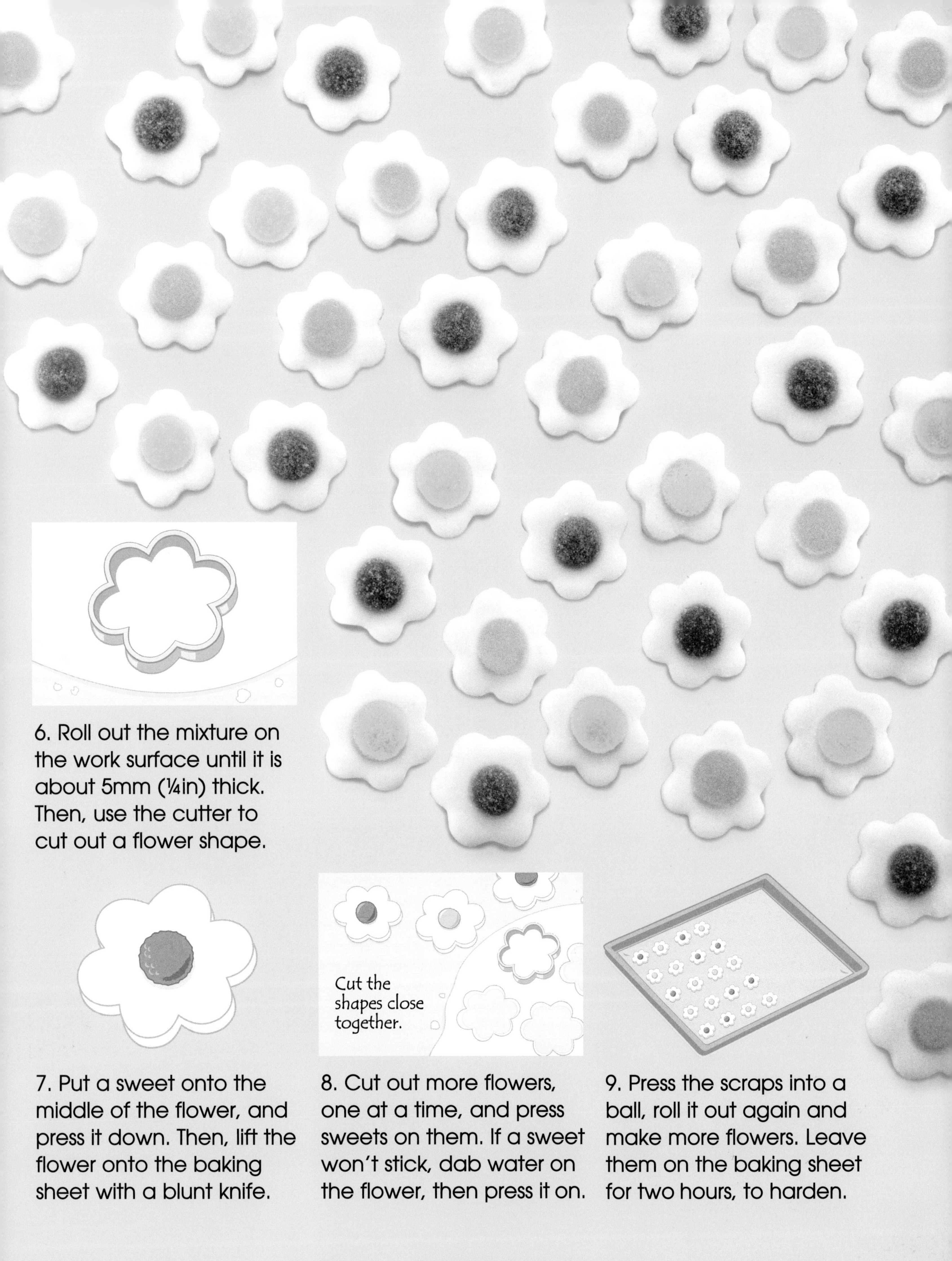

6. Roll out the mixture on the work surface until it is about 5mm (¼in) thick. Then, use the cutter to cut out a flower shape.

7. Put a sweet onto the middle of the flower, and press it down. Then, lift the flower onto the baking sheet with a blunt knife.

8. Cut out more flowers, one at a time, and press sweets on them. If a sweet won't stick, dab water on the flower, then press it on.

9. Press the scraps into a ball, roll it out again and make more flowers. Leave them on the baking sheet for two hours, to harden.

Sticky Easter cakes

This recipe is based on cakes that are traditionally eaten in Greece at Easter.

To make eight cakes, you will need:

100g (4oz) soft light brown sugar
100g (4oz) butter, softened
2 medium eggs
2 teaspoons baking powder
100g (4oz) semolina
½ teaspoon of ground cinnamon
100g (4oz) ground almonds*
4 tablespoons lemon juice (from a bottle or squeezed from a lemon)
a 12-hole muffin tin

For the orange and lemon syrup:
1 small orange
1 tablespoon of lemon juice (from a bottle or squeezed from a lemon)
4 tablespoons golden syrup

You could serve the cakes with Greek yogurt and fresh orange segments.

Heat your oven to 200°C, 400°F, gas mark 6, before you start.

The cakes need to be stored in an airtight container and eaten within three days. Don't pour the syrup over them more than two hours before serving.

Use a pastry brush.

1. Brush some oil inside eight of the muffin holes. Cut a small circle of baking parchment to put in the bottom of each.

2. Put the sugar and the butter into a large bowl. Beat them together until they are mixed well and look creamy.

* Don't give these to anyone who is allergic to nuts.

3. Break the eggs into a small bowl and beat them. Stir in the beaten eggs, a little at a time, to the creamy mixture.

4. Mix the baking powder, semolina, cinnamon and almonds in a large bowl. Add them, and the lemon juice, to the mixture.

5. Mix everything well, then spoon the mixture into the holes in the tin. Bake the cakes in the oven for about 15 minutes.

The tin will still be hot.

6. Carefully lift the cakes out of the oven. Leave them in the tin for a minute, then loosen their sides with a blunt knife.

7. Turn the cakes onto a large plate to cool. Then, carefully peel the baking parchment circles off each one.

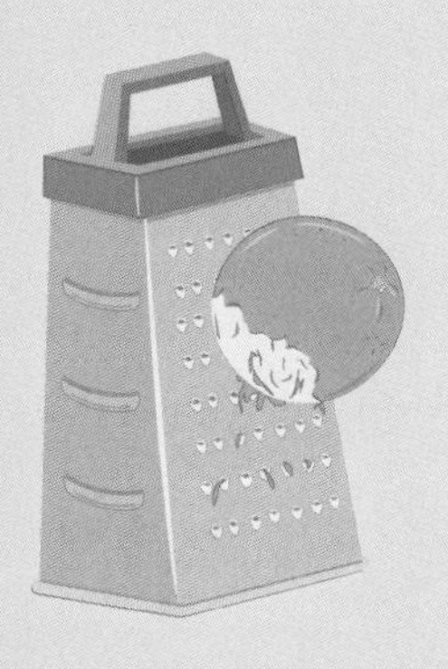

8. For the syrup, grate some rind from about half of the orange on the fine holes on a grater. Put the rind into a small pan.

9. Cut the orange in half. Squeeze out the juice, using a lemon squeezer, and add 2 tablespoons of juice to the pan.

10. Add the lemon juice and golden syrup. Over a very low heat, gently warm the mixture, stirring it all the time.

11. When the mixture is runny, use a teaspoon to trickle it over the cakes. Let the mixture cool a little before serving.

Sunshine toast

You will need:

margarine
1 slice of bread
1 small or medium egg
a large cookie cutter
a baking sheet

Heat your oven to 200°C, 400°F, gas mark 6, before you start.

The toast needs to be eaten as soon as it's cooked.

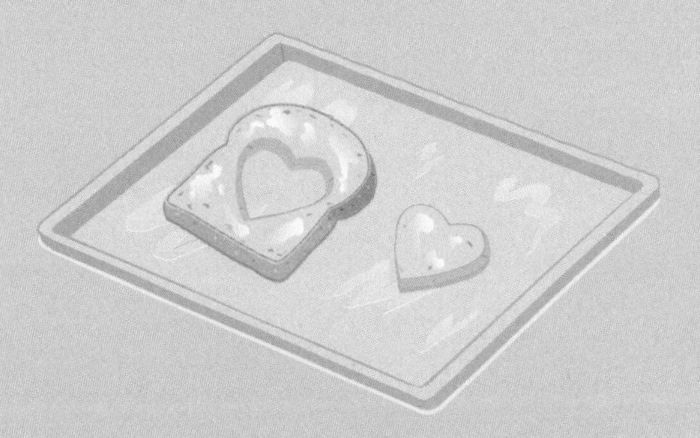

1. Dip a paper towel into some margarine. Then, rub margarine all over the baking sheet, to grease it.

2. Using a knife, spread margarine on one side of the slice of bread. Then, press the cutter into the middle of the bread.

3. Lift out the shape you have cut out. Put both pieces of bread onto the baking sheet, with their margarine sides upwards.

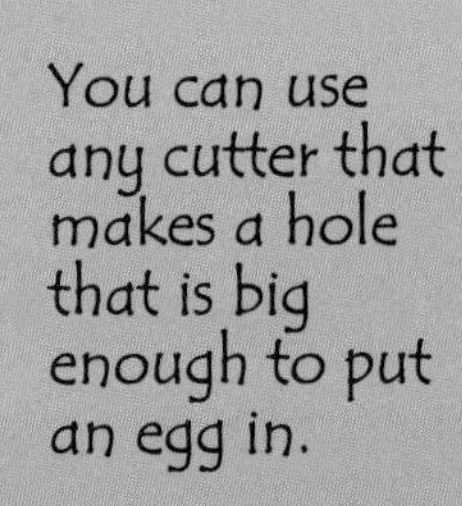

You can use any cutter that makes a hole that is big enough to put an egg in.

4. Break the egg onto a saucer. Then, carefully slide the egg into the hole in the bread. Put the baking sheet in the oven.

5. Bake the bread and egg in the oven for seven minutes, or for a little longer if you don't like a runny egg yolk.

Use a fish slice.

6. Wearing oven gloves, carefully lift the baking sheet out of the oven. Then, lift the pieces of toast onto a plate.

Easter truffles

To make 12 truffles, you will need:

225g (8oz) white, milk or plain chocolate drops
4 tablespoons double cream
1 teaspoon of vanilla essence
about 4 tablespoons sugar strands
small paper cases

The truffles need to be stored in an airtight container in a fridge. Eat them within five days.

1. Pour about 3cm (1in) of water into a pan. Heat the pan until the water bubbles, then remove the pan from the heat.

2. Put the chocolate drops and cream into a heatproof bowl. Using oven gloves, carefully put the bowl into the pan.

3. Stir the chocolate and cream with a wooden spoon until the chocolate has melted. Carefully lift the bowl out of the water.

4. Leave the bowl to cool for 20 minutes, then stir in the vanilla. Put the mixture in a fridge for 1½ hours, until it is very firm.

5. Put the sugar strands onto a plate. Scoop up some chocolate mixture with a teaspoon and put it into the sugar strands.

6. Using your fingers, roll the spoonful in the strands to make a ball. When it is covered, put it in a paper case. Make more truffles.

7. Put the truffles onto a plate, then put them in the fridge for 30 minutes, until they are completely hard. Keep them in the fridge.

To make truffle eggs, squash the spoonful of mixture slightly when you roll it in the sugar strands.

Marzipan animals and eggs

To make 4 chicks, 3 rabbits and lots of eggs and carrots, you will need:

250g (9oz) pack of marzipan*
yellow and red food colouring
toothpicks

The animals and eggs need to be stored in an airtight container and eaten within three weeks.

Chicks

Wrap one half in plastic foodwrap.

1. Unwrap the marzipan and cut it in half. Put one half in a small bowl and add 12 drops of yellow food colouring.

2. Mix the colouring in with your fingers until the marzipan is completely yellow. Then, cut the piece of marzipan in half.

3. Put one half in a bowl and mix in a drop of red colouring. If the marzipan isn't bright orange, add another drop of red.

Keep this piece for the wings.

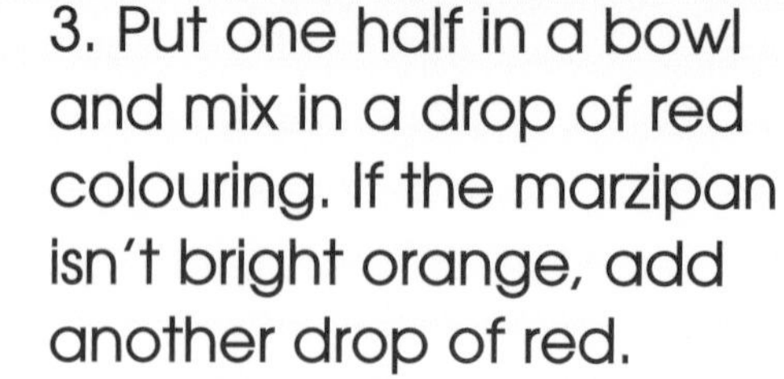

Press in two eyes with a toothpick.

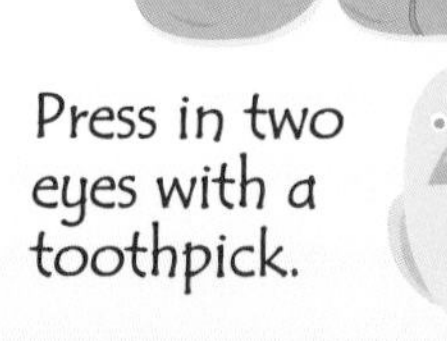

4. Cut the yellow marzipan into five pieces. Make four of them into balls. Then, squeeze them at one end to make tear shapes.

5. Make eight small yellow wings and press two onto each body. Then, roll a beak from orange marzipan and press it on.

6. For the feet, make a tiny orange ball and flatten it. Cut the shape halfway across and open it out. Press a chick on top.

* Marzipan contains ground nuts, so don't give these to anyone who is allergic to nuts.

Rabbits

Use plastic foodwrap.

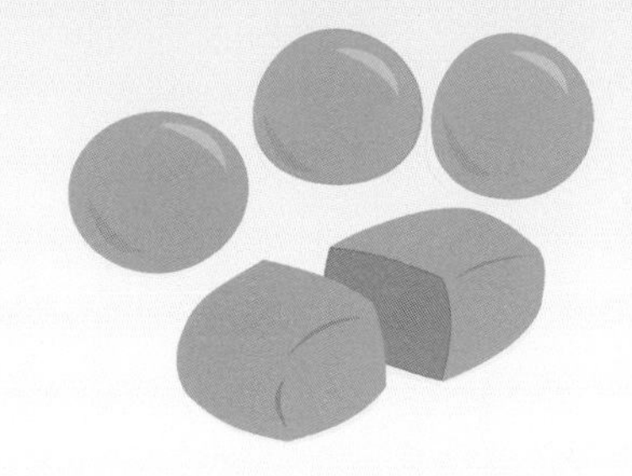

1. Unwrap the plain marzipan. Mix one drop of red colouring into it to make pink. Cut it in half and wrap one half.

2. Cut the unwrapped piece in half. With one half, make three balls, for the bodies. Then, cut the other piece in half.

3. From one half, roll three smaller balls, for the heads. Then, make six ears, three tails and three noses from the other half.

If the ears won't stick, dip the ends in water.

4. Pinch each ear to make a fold. Press ears, a head, nose and tail onto each body. Then, press in eyes with a toothpick.

Marbled eggs

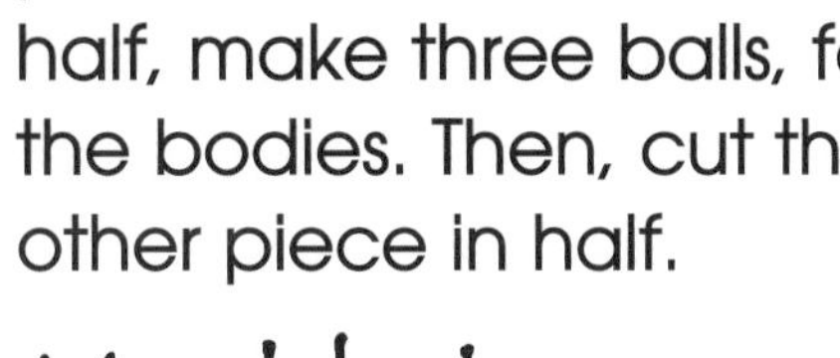

1. Unwrap the second piece of pink marzipan. Add a drop of red colouring, and start to mix it in with your hands.

2. Stop mixing in the colouring when the marzipan looks marbled. Roll the marzipan into lots of little egg shapes.

Use orange marzipan to make carrots. Make marks on them with a blunt knife.

Press a rabbit's head on the front of its body, to make it look as if it is lying down.

Easter fudge

To make 36 pieces of fudge, you will need:

450g (1lb) icing sugar, preferably unrefined
100g (4oz) white marshmallows
2 tablespoons milk
100g (4oz) unsalted butter
half a teaspoon of vanilla essence
2 drops of yellow food colouring
a shallow 18cm (7in) square cake tin

The fudge needs to be stored in an airtight container in a fridge and eaten within a week.

Find out how to wrap your fudge like this on page 30.

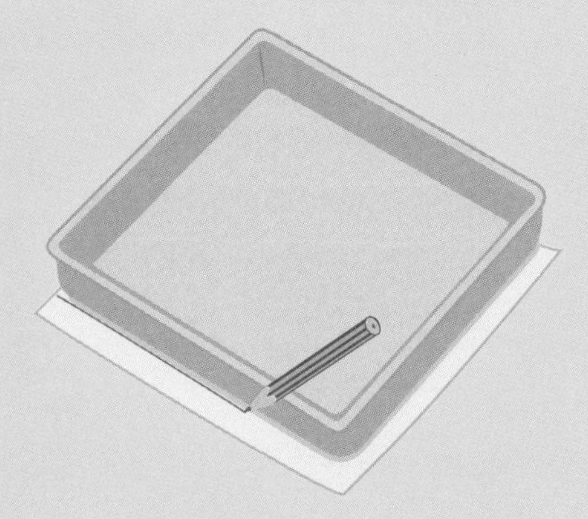

1. Put the tin onto a piece of greaseproof paper. Using a pencil, draw around the tin and cut out the square.

2. Using a paper towel, wipe some oil onto the sides and bottom of the tin. Press in the paper square and wipe it too.

3. Sift the icing sugar through a sieve into a large bowl. Make a small hollow in the middle of the sugar with a spoon.

4. Using clean scissors, cut the marshmallows in half and put them in a small pan. Add the milk, butter and vanilla essence.

5. Gently heat the pan. Stir the mixture every now and then with a wooden spoon until everything has melted.

Use a spoon.

6. Pour the mixture into the hollow in the sugar. Beat everything together until it is smooth, then mix in the food colouring.

Smooth the top with the back of a spoon.

7. Put the fudge into the tin and push it into the corners. When it is cool, put it in a fridge for three hours to go firm.

8. Loosen the edges of the fudge with a blunt knife, then turn it out onto a chopping board. Remove the paper.

9. Cut the fudge into 36 pieces. Then, put the pieces in an airtight container in the fridge for an hour to harden.

To make pink fudge, use pink marshmallows and add a drop of red or pink food colouring.

Coloured eggs

To make six coloured eggs, you will need:

6 eggs, at room temperature
food colouring
wax crayons
tiny star-shaped stickers
rubber bands

The eggs need to be stored in a fridge and eaten within three days. They can be eaten with a fresh mixed salad or on their own.

Cooking the eggs

1. Put the eggs into a pan of cold water. Heat the pan until the water is gently boiling, then reduce the heat a little.

2. Cook the eggs for eight to nine minutes. Lift out one egg at a time. Cool them in a bowl of cold water for ten minutes.

Wax patterns

1. Using a wax crayon, draw patterns on a dry egg. Then, put 3-4 teaspoons of bright food colouring into a glass.

2. Half fill the glass with water, then put the egg into the glass. Using a spoon, turn the egg to colour it all over.

3. When the egg is brightly coloured, lift it out of the glass with a spoon. Put the egg on a paper towel to dry.

Stickers

1. Press tiny stickers onto an egg. Use shiny ones if you can, because they don't soak up so much food colouring.

2. Colour the egg in a glass, as you did before. Then, lift the egg out with a spoon and put it on a paper towel to dry.

3. When the colouring is dry, peel off the stickers. You'll see the colour of the eggshell where the stickers were.

These rabbits and chicks were painted straight onto the eggs with food colouring.

Stripes

1. Stretch a short, thick rubber band around a dry egg. Then, stretch one around the egg from the top to the bottom.

2. Add lots more rubber bands, then colour the egg and let it dry. Then, remove the rubber bands to see stripes of eggshell.

Easter cake

You will need:

225g (8oz) self-raising flour
1 teaspoon of baking powder
4 medium eggs
225g (8oz) caster sugar
225g (8oz) soft margarine
two round 20cm (8in) cake tins

For the butter icing:
225g (8oz) icing sugar
100g (4oz) unsalted butter, softened
1 tablespoon of milk
1 teaspoon of vanilla essence

Heat your oven to 180°C, 350°F, gas mark 4, before you start.

The cake needs to be stored in an airtight container in a cool place and eaten within three days.

To make the icing yellow, add a teaspoon of yellow food colouring at step 8.

Decorate the cake with flower sweets (pages 4-5) and marzipan chicks (pages 12-13).

1. Put the cake tins onto a piece of greaseproof paper and draw around them. Cut out the circles, just inside the line.

2. Wipe the sides and bottoms of the tins with a little oil. Put the paper circles inside and wipe them with a little oil too.

3. Using a sieve, sift the flour and baking powder into a large bowl. Then, carefully break the eggs into a cup.

4. Add the eggs, sugar and margarine to the bowl. Beat everything with a wooden spoon until they are mixed well.

5. Put half of the mixture into each tin. Smooth the tops with the back of a spoon. Then, bake the cakes for 25 minutes.

6. Press the cakes with a finger. If they are cooked, they will spring back. Let them cool a little, then put them on a wire rack.

7. Peel the paper off the cakes and leave them to cool. When the cakes are cold, sift the icing sugar into a bowl.

8. Add the butter, milk and vanilla. Stir the ingredients together, then beat them until the mixture is fluffy. Put one cake on a plate.

9. Spread the cake with half of the icing. Then, put the other cake on top and spread it with the rest of the icing.

Chocolate nests

To make 10 nests, you will need:

225g (8oz) plain chocolate
50g (2oz) butter
2 tablespoons golden syrup
100g (4oz) corn flakes
30 chocolate mini eggs
paper cake cases
a baking tray with shallow pans

The nests need to be stored in an airtight container in a fridge. Eat them within three days.

1. Put ten paper cases into pans in the baking tray. Break the chocolate into squares and put them in a large pan.

2. Add the butter to the pan. Dip a tablespoon in some hot water, then use the spoon to add the golden syrup.

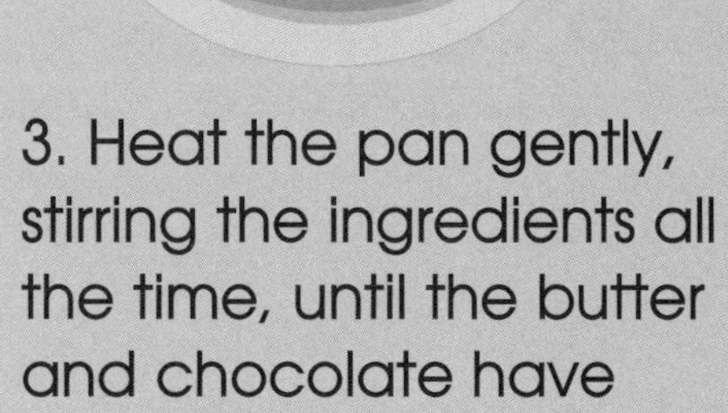

3. Heat the pan gently, stirring the ingredients all the time, until the butter and chocolate have completely melted.

4. Turn off the heat, then add the corn flakes to the pan. Gently stir them into the chocolate, until they are coated all over.

Push the flakes up the sides.

5. Fill the paper cases with the mixture. Using the back of a teaspoon, make a hollow in the middle of each nest.

6. Arrange three mini eggs in each nest. Then, put the tray in the fridge and leave it for about an hour to set.

7. Take the nests out of the paper cases and put them on a plate. Keep them in the fridge until you want to eat them.

Easter fruit bread

To make a loaf with about 12 slices, you will need:

225g (8oz) strong plain flour
½ teaspoon of ground mixed spice
½ teaspoon of salt
25g (1oz) butter
1 tablespoon of caster sugar
2 teaspoons easy-blend dried yeast
1 medium egg and 5 tablespoons milk, beaten together
100g (4oz) luxury dried mixed fruit
a little milk for brushing
a 20.5 x 12.5 x 8cm (8 x 5 x 3½in) loaf tin

For the icing:
50g (2oz) icing sugar
1 tablespoon of lemon juice (from a bottle or squeezed from a lemon)
50g (2oz) chopped glacé cherries

Heat your oven to 200°C, 400°F, gas mark 6.

Easter fruit bread needs to be stored in an airtight container and eaten within three days.

Draw around the bottom of the tin.

1. Put the tin onto baking parchment. Draw around it and cut out the shape. Grease the tin and put the paper in the bottom.

2. Sift the flour, mixed spice and salt through a sieve into a large bowl. Cut the butter into cubes and add it to the bowl.

3. Using your fingertips, rub in the butter until the mixture looks like breadcrumbs. Stir in the caster sugar and yeast.

4. Pour the beaten egg mixture into the bowl. Stir everything with a wooden spoon until you make a dough.

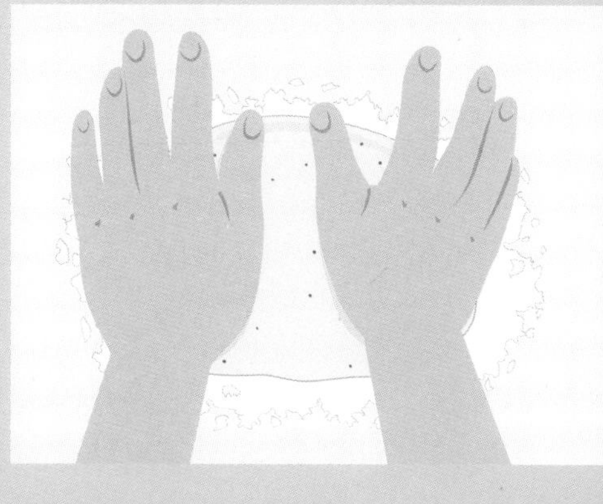

5. Sprinkle some flour onto a clean, dry work surface. Then, knead the dough by pushing it away from you with both hands.

6. Fold the dough in half and turn it around. Push it away again. Do this for five minutes, then put it into a greased bowl.

7. Cover the bowl with plastic foodwrap. Leave it in a warm place for an hour, until the dough has risen to twice its size.

8. Turn the dough out of the bowl and sprinkle the dried fruit over it. Knead the fruit into the dough until it is mixed in.

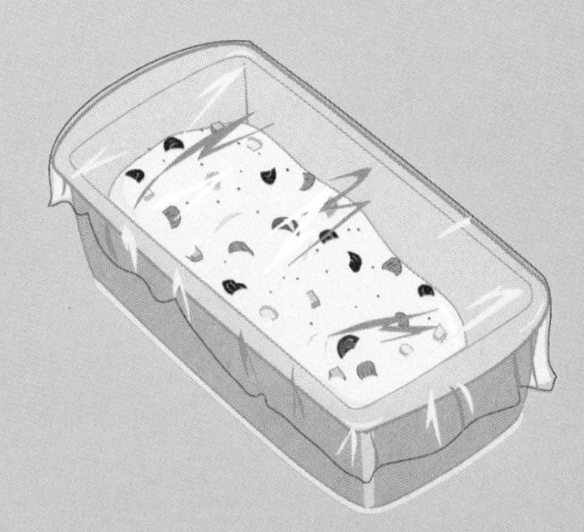

9. Put the dough in the tin and cover the tin with plastic foodwrap. Put it in a warm place for about 45 minutes to rise some more.

10. Heat your oven. Brush the top of the dough with milk, then put the tin in the oven and bake the bread for 30-35 minutes.

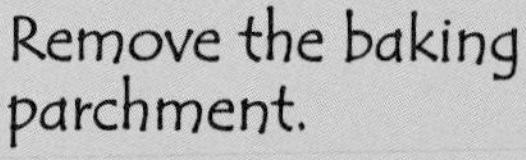

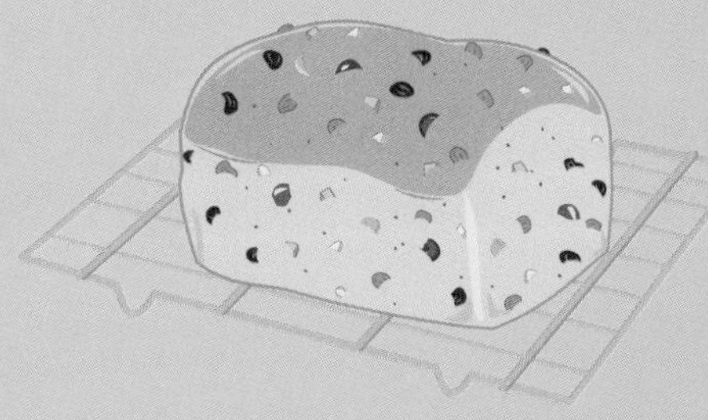

11. Push a skewer into the loaf. If it comes out clean, the loaf is cooked. Take the loaf out of the tin. Put it on a wire rack to cool.

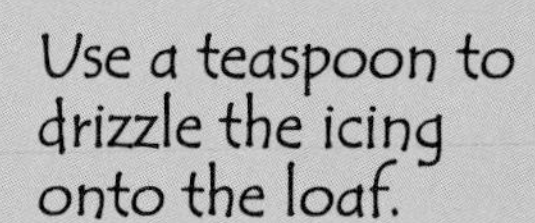

12. Sift the icing sugar into a bowl and mix in the lemon juice. Drizzle the icing over the loaf, then scatter the cherries on top.

Spiced Easter biscuits

To make about 25 biscuits, you will need:

1 medium egg
100g (4oz) butter, softened
75g (3oz) caster sugar
200g (7oz) plain flour
½ teaspoon of ground cinnamon
½ teaspoon of ground ginger
50g (2oz) currants
5 teaspoons milk
about 2 tablespoons caster sugar

a 6cm (2½in) fluted cookie cutter
two greased baking sheets

Heat your oven to 200°C, 400°F, gas mark 6.

The biscuits need to be stored in an airtight container and eaten within five days.

Find out how to make cellophane bags for your biscuits on page 31.

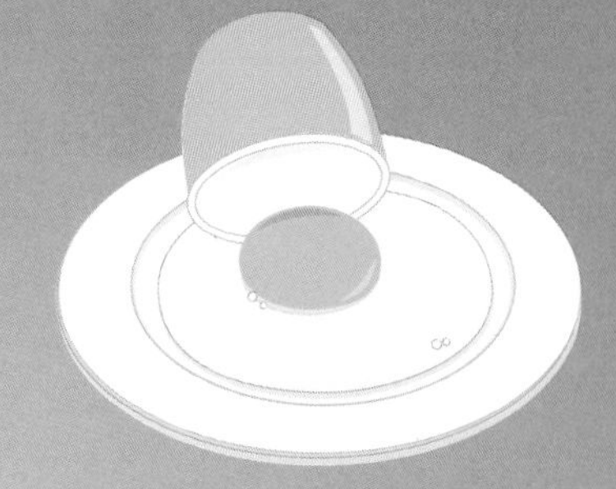

1. Carefully break the egg on the edge of a small bowl, and pour it slowly onto a saucer. Then, put an egg cup over the yolk.

You will use the egg white later.

2. Hold the egg cup over the yolk and tip the saucer over the small bowl, so that the egg white dribbles into it.

Use a wooden spoon.

3. Put the butter and sugar into a large bowl and beat them until they are creamy. Then, add the egg yolk and beat it in.

4. Using a sieve, sift the flour, cinnamon and ginger into the bowl. Then, add the currants and the milk too.

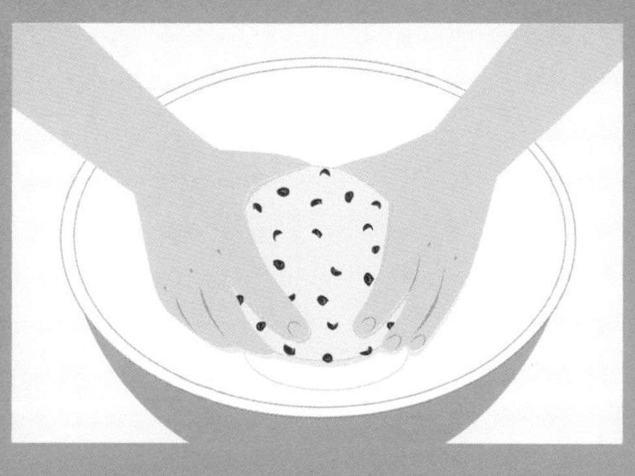

5. Mix everything together with a spoon, then squeeze the mixture with your hands until you have made a dough.

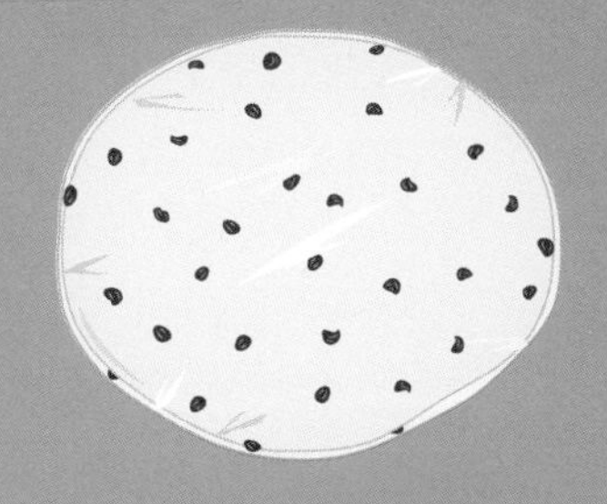

6. Wrap the dough in plastic foodwrap. Put it in the fridge for 20 minutes. Then, sprinkle a clean work surface with flour.

7. Heat your oven. Then, put the dough onto the work surface and roll it out until it is about 5mm (¼in) thick.

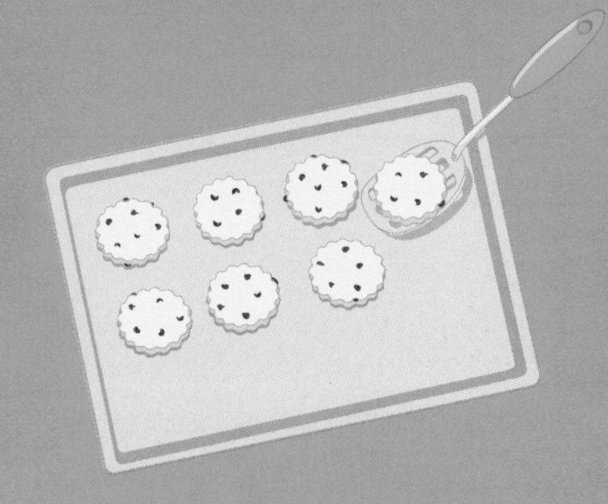

8. Use the cutter to cut out lots of biscuits. Then, carefully lift the biscuits onto the baking sheets, using a fish slice.

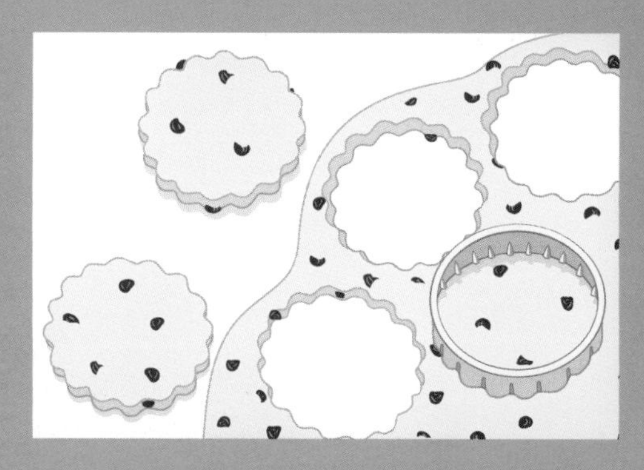

9. Squeeze the scraps of dough together to make a ball. Then, roll the dough out as you did before and cut out more biscuits.

10. Using a fork, beat the egg white for a few seconds until it is frothy. Brush a little egg white on the top of each biscuit.

11. Sprinkle a little caster sugar over each biscuit. Bake them in the oven for 12-15 minutes. They will turn golden brown.

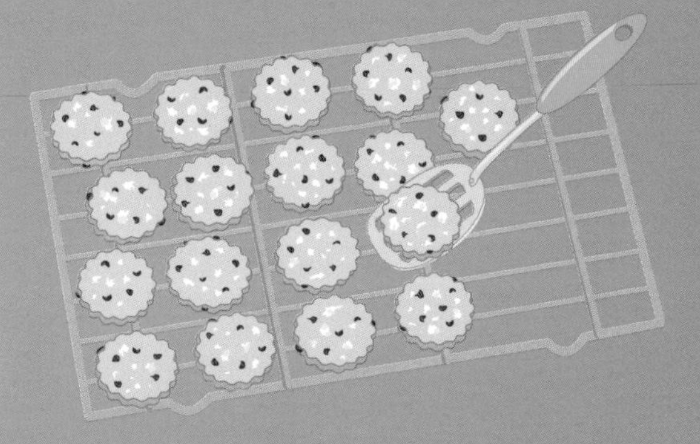

12. Leave the biscuits on the baking sheets for about five minutes. Then, lift them onto a wire rack and leave them to cool.

Easter daisy biscuits

To make about 30 biscuits, you will need:

75g (3oz) icing sugar
150g (5oz) butter, softened
a lemon
225g (8oz) plain flour
writing icing
small sweets and silver cake-decorating balls
a flower-shaped cookie cutter
two greased baking sheets

Heat your oven to 180°C, 350°F, gas mark 4.

The biscuits need to be stored in an airtight container and eaten within three days.

Use a sieve.

1. Sift the icing sugar into a large bowl. Add the butter and mix everything together with a spoon until the mixture is creamy.

2. Grate the rind from the lemon using the medium holes on a grater. Then, add the rind to the bowl and mix everything again.

Use a lemon squeezer.

3. Cut the lemon in half and squeeze the juice from it. Then, stir a tablespoon of lemon juice into the creamy mixture.

4. Sift the flour through a sieve into the bowl. Mix it in until you make a smooth dough. Then, wrap the dough in plastic foodwrap.

Sprinkle some flour on a rolling pin too.

5. Put the dough in a fridge for 30 minutes, to become firmer. Then, sprinkle some flour onto a clean work surface.

6. Heat your oven. Then, roll out the dough until it is about 5mm (¼in) thick. Cut out lots of flower shapes, using the cutter.

This recipe makes 30 biscuits this size. The number of biscuits depends on the size of your cutter.

7. Put the flower shapes onto the baking sheets. Squeeze the scraps into a ball, then roll it out again and cut out more shapes.

The biscuits should be lightly browned.

8. Bake the biscuits for 15 minutes. Leave them on the baking sheets for two minutes, then put them on a wire rack to cool.

9. When the biscuits are cool, decorate them with icing. Draw lines, swirls and dots. Press sweets into the middle of the icing.

Cheesy chicks

To make about 15 chicks, you will need:

75g (3oz) mature Cheddar cheese
100g (4oz) plain flour
50g (2oz) butter, refrigerated
the yolk from a medium egg
5 teaspoons cold water
a chick-shaped or other cookie cutter
two greased baking sheets

Heat your oven to 190°C, 375°F, gas mark 5.

The chicks need to be stored in an airtight container and eaten within four days.

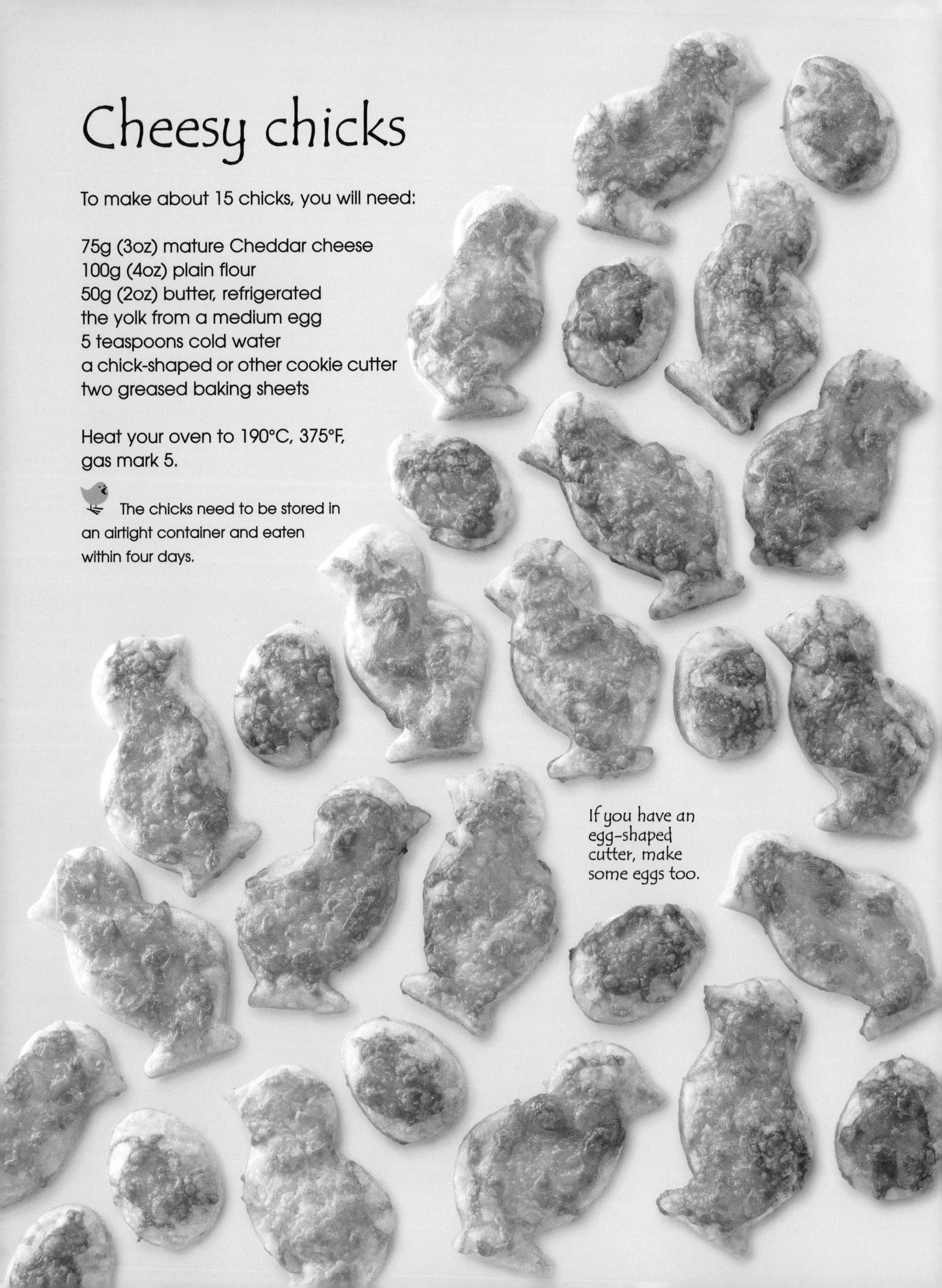

If you have an egg-shaped cutter, make some eggs too.

Use the fine holes on a grater.

1. Grate the cheese. Sift the flour through a sieve into a large bowl. Then, cut the butter into chunks and add it to the bowl.

2. Mix in the butter until it is coated in flour. Rub it in with your fingers, until it looks like breadcrumbs. Add half of the cheese.

3. Mix the egg yolk and water in a small bowl. Put two teaspoonfuls in a cup, then pour the rest over the flour mixture.

4. Stir everything together, then squeeze the mixture until you make a smooth dough. Make it a slightly flattened round shape.

5. Wrap the dough in plastic foodwrap and put it in a fridge to chill for 30 minutes. While it is in the fridge, heat your oven.

6. Sprinkle flour onto a clean work surface and a rolling pin. Roll out the dough until it is about 5mm (¼in) thick.

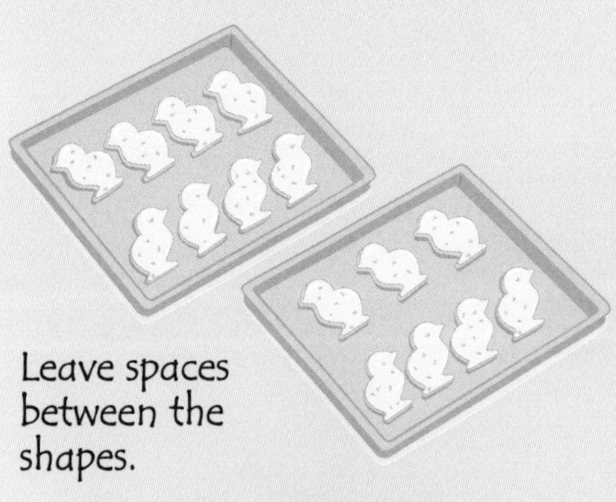

Leave spaces between the shapes.

Use a fish slice.

7. Use the cutter to cut out chick shapes. Put them onto the baking sheets. Squeeze the scraps into a ball, then roll them out.

8. Cut out more shapes. Brush the tops of the shapes with the egg mixture, then sprinkle them with grated cheese.

9. Bake the chicks for 12 minutes. Leave them on the baking sheets for five minutes, then put them on a wire rack to cool.

Wrapping ideas

Bunny boxes

This side of the head needs to be on the fold.

1. Carefully cut the top off a tissue box and paint the box. Find a piece of thick paper the same colour. Fold the paper in half.

2. Draw half of a bunny's head, like this. Keeping the paper folded, cut out the shape. Open out the paper and flatten it.

3. Draw a face. Then, glue the head onto one end of the box. Glue a piece of cotton wool onto the opposite end, for a tail.

Pretty sweets

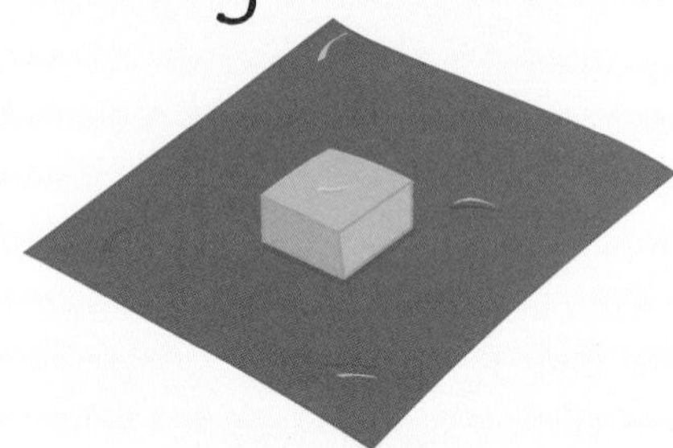

1. Cut a square of thin cellophane that is bigger than the sweet, like this. Then, put the sweet in the middle of the square.

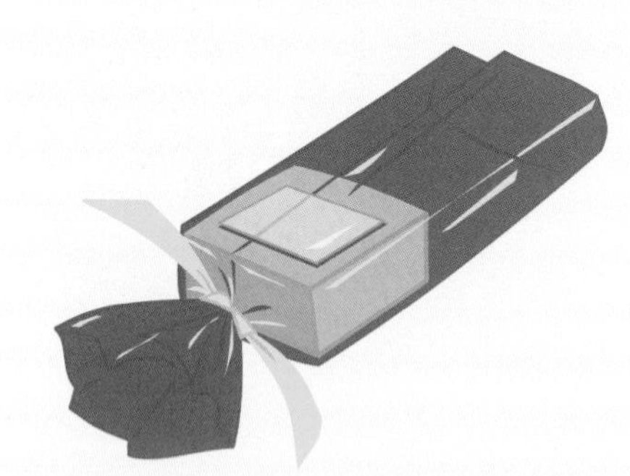

2. Wrap the cellophane around the sweet and tape it. Tie a piece of parcel ribbon around each end of the sweet.

Pile sweets or biscuits into a bunny box as an Easter gift.

Sweetie bags

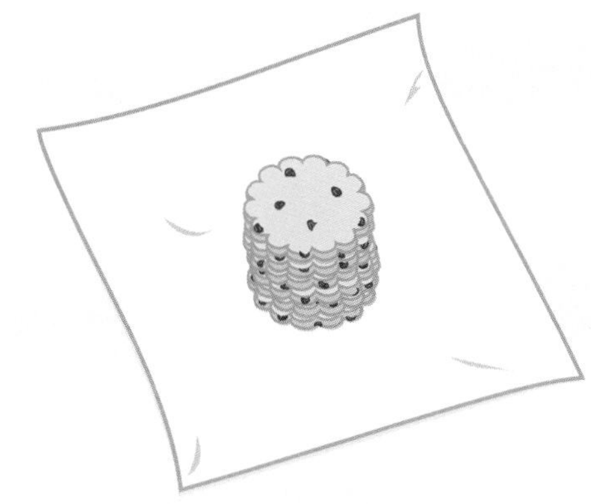

1. Cut a square of thin cellophane. Then, put several biscuits or some sweets in the middle of the square.

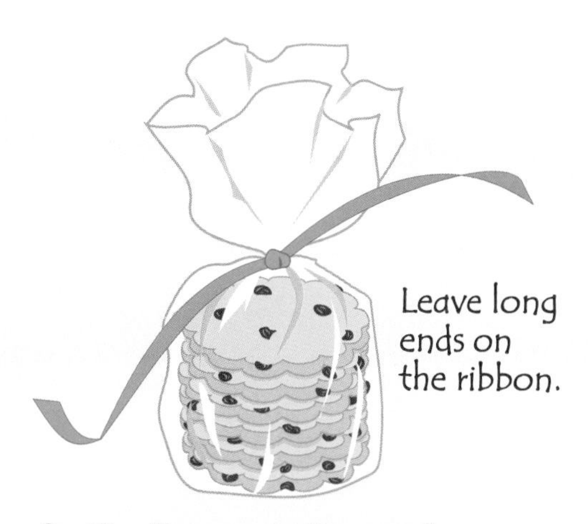

Leave long ends on the ribbon.

2. Gather up the edges of the square and tie a piece of parcel ribbon around the cellophane, above the biscuits.

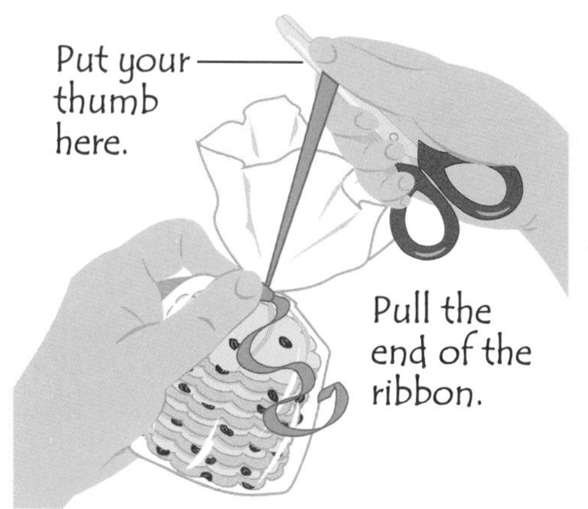

Put your thumb here.

Pull the end of the ribbon.

3. To make the ribbon curl, hold it between your thumb and the blade of some closed scissors, and pull it firmly.

Add a paper handle to a box to make a basket.

Save food boxes and wrap ribbons around them.

Easter tags

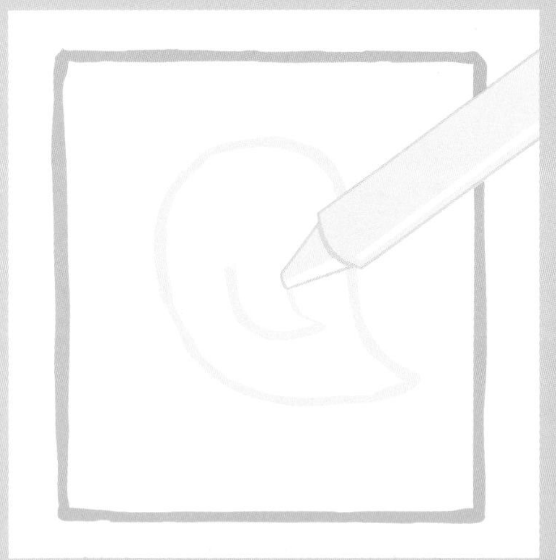

1. Draw a rectangle on a piece of white card with a wax crayon. Then, draw the body of a chick with a yellow crayon.

2. Add a beak, a leg and an eye. Paint over the picture with runny paint. The crayon lines will show through the paint.

3. When the paint is dry, cut around the rectangle, leaving a painted edge. Tape a piece of ribbon to the back of the tag.

Draw an egg shape and fill it with lines and patterns.

You can fill different areas with different colours of paint, like this flower.

Series editor: Fiona Watt • Managing designer: Mary Cartwright • Photographic manipulation: Emma Julings
This edition published in 2008, Usborne Publishing Ltd, Usborne House, 83-85 Saffron Hill, London, EC1N 8RT. www.usborne.com
Printed in Malaysia.